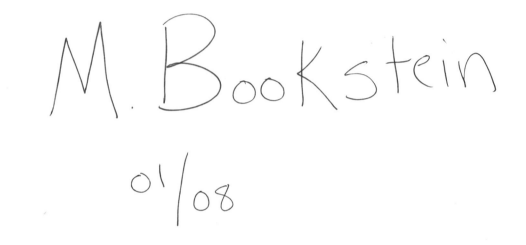

M. Bookstein

01/08

This book belongs to:

1

With great pride and with hope for tomorrow,
we invite you to join us
in the celebration of

Alfie's Bark Mitzvah™

Saturday, the twenty-fourth of May

at nine o'clock in the morning

Sitstay Shalom Temple

27 Happy Barkers Boulevard

Canine Corners, Arizona

A luncheon reception will follow

RSVP

Little Five Star

www.AlfiesBarkMitzvah.com

P.O. Box 6698

Chandler, AZ 85246-6698

(480) 940-8182

Linda F. Radke, President
Little Five Star, a division of Five Star Publications, Inc.
PO Box 6698
Chandler, AZ 85246-6698

480-940-8182

www.alfiesbarkmitzvah.com

Library of Congress Cataloging-in-Publication Data

Cohen, Shari.
   Alfie's bark mitzvah / by Shari Cohen ; songs by Marcelo Gindlin.
      p. cm.
   Summary: In a small synagogue, surrounded by his loving family, Alfie completes the ceremony that marks his passage from being a puppy to a dog.
   ISBN-13: 978-1-58985-055-2
   ISBN-10: 1-58985-055-6
   [1. Bar mitzvah--Fiction. 2. Judaism--Customs and practices--Fiction. 3. Jews--Fiction. 4. Dogs--Fiction. 5. Stories in rhyme.] I. Gindlin, Marcelo. II. Title.
   PZ8.3.C6643Alf 2007
   [E]--dc22
                         2006033419

PRINTED IN ISRAEL

Editor: Paul Howey
Cover & Interior Design: Linda Longmire
Project Manager: Sue DeFabis

Acknowledgements

This book was written with humor and light spirit, while embracing tradition and song.

Thank you to my cousin Cantor Jay Frailich, who was joking one day when he gave me two words to write a new story about—Bark Mitzvah. He had since forgotten, but I didn't. And so began the creation of our beloved Alfie. Today, surrounded by family and friends this puppy with a Jewish soul has proceeded on a heart-building journey.

I would like to thank my husband Paul, who was the guiding force behind this book. I couldn't have done it without you.

Many thanks to my publisher Linda Radke for your dedication and enthusiasm. You have been incredible to work with.

And to the hardworking Little Five Star team:
Editor Paul Howey, Project Manager Sue DeFabis, and Graphic Designer Linda Longmire for your creative talents and expertise in bringing this project together.

To my mom Harriet, and my children Barry, Adam and Stephanie—a special thanks for your support and patience, taking time to read and comment on the story I shared with you as it was progressing.

Gratitude to Nadia Komorova for your brilliant pages of art and for magically bringing our characters to life.

And a special thanks to Cantor Marcelo Gindlin—for your voice, your soul and your friendship.

Shari

Acknowledgements

I would like to acknowledge the persons who encouraged and inspired me to go forward with my dream of bringing joy through music to children everywhere:

Troy Dexter, the most caring professional and talented musician, producer, and friend for helping bring this project to completion.

My family and especially my sister Cantor Mariana Gindlin for their continuous love and support.

Everyone involved in creating this project—Dr. Michael Graubert for his love and inspiration; Chaplain Judith Sommerstein for her editorial contribution and support; Diana Sztejnbok and Batia Rogovsky for being with me in every step of my life; Tova Morcos, my extraordinary voice coach, for her uplifting help; vocalists Cantor Ruti Braier, Sue Epstein, Cantorial Soloist Lonee Frailich, Cantorial Soloist Lorna Lembeck, Jamie Rice, Cantor Wally Schachet-Briskin, and Ditza Zakay; and the children's choir from the Malibu Jewish Center & Synagogue.

My gratitude to Rabbi Judith HaLevy and the Malibu Jewish Center & Synagogue community for their support. And finally Shari and Paul Cohen for their friendship and faith in me.

Cantor Marcelo Gindlin

Alfie's Bark Mitzvah™

By Shari Cohen
with Songs by Cantor Marcelo Gindlin

Illustrations by Nadia Komorova

It was quite a Bark Mitzvah
In a small synagogue
That day Alfie passed
From being a puppy to a dog.

8

Friends and family gathered
From New York and Delaware

From Israel and Argentina
They arrived by land, sea and air.

ALFIE'S
5 miles

Jose and Diego
Aunt Rose and Uncle Lev

Joined Cousin Rachel
And twins Ziv and Zev.

All the cooking and baking
Left no time to play —

14

Everyone was getting ready
For Alfie's big day.

Shhhhhhh...

Soon there stood Alfie
Beaming and quite proud ...
Then he began singing
In a voice clear and loud.

"Baruch ..."

He stopped just a moment
For his heart beat with fright —
So many songs and so many prayers

Will I ever get it right?

19

But sitting right in front
And watching him with pride

Were Bubbie and Zayde
With smiles oh so wide.

He smiled back at them...

"It will be okay," he sighed.

Alfie sang
the morning blessing
Through each
and every part

With joy in his words
And music in his heart.

His voice traveled outside
And went for miles around

Others stopped to listen
When they heard his beautiful sound.

Inside, the chanting and the prayers
Were a cause for celebration

A gift handed down
To each new generation.

A new meaning of life
Now came Alfie's way
The passing down of tradition
On this his special day.

31

Then Zayde's eyes twinkled
"I'd like you all to note
The thoughtfulness of
Alfie's own mitzvot."

"He visits the sick

He spends time with the old

And the lonely who simply
Want a kind paw to hold."

"He gives without asking
Always doing his part

Alfie cares for others
With kindness and with heart."

Holding his head high
Alfie shared his heartfelt goal,
"To be truthful and forgiving,
And to have a loving soul."

"To study," he said "and
To become knowing and wise
And to try and see the world
Through someone else's eyes."

The room became quiet
When in a voice rich and fine
Alfie gave the blessing
Over a biscuit and some wine.

Then Uncle Lev stood
And chuckled with a grin,

"The ceremony is over, Now let the party begin!"

"Join cousins Ari and Ben
Miriam and Dora —
Everyone on the floor
It's time to dance the hora!"

"Gather for pictures
Now smile everyone —

Watch him open presents and then
Let's all have some fun!"

Soon the day had ended
And after the last shalom
A happy but tired Alfie
Walked slowly to his home.

As he drifted off to sleep
Alfie was quite proud
Of the job he had done
For he was now a Bark Mitzvah

And on a journey just begun!

MAZAL TOV!

About the Author

Shari Cohen is the author of fourteen books for children and young adults. She also works as a journalist for several national magazines. Her stories have appeared in *Family Circle*, *Woman's World*, and *Woman's Day*. She is also a contributor to the *Chicken Soup for the Soul* series.

About collaborating with Cantor Gindlin — Cantor Gindlin moved next door and it wasn't long before I heard his voice coming through his window as he practiced for the High Holiday Services. We soon became friends and talked often of our work and our desire to create material for children. We decided to work together on a book with songs to accompany the story.

About the Cantor

Cantor Marcelo Gindlin was born in Buenos Aires, Argentina and has lived in southern California for seven years where he is the full-time Cantor of the Malibu Jewish Center & Synagogue. In addition to his certification as Hazzan & Ba'al Tefillah from the Latin American Rabbinical Seminary, he has two degrees in music therapy and has extensive experience as a teacher, composer, choir director, and performer.

About collaborating with Shari Cohen — When Shari told me about her idea for a book about a dog with a Jewish soul, I began singing a tune for *Alfie's Bark Mitzvah*™. We felt it would be a great story. And the journey began...

About the Illustrator

Nadia Komorova was born in Czechoslovakia. She studied at the Academy of Fine Arts and Design in Bratislava, Slovakia, where she also received instruction in classical piano (the music of the piano continues to fill her studio as she creates her paintings). Nadia has an insatiable curiosity about the colors of light reflected in nature. In fact, her favorite interests are light that we cannot see but which is all essential for capturing on canvas the subjects of her paintings. She is intrigued by each of her subjects, drawn to their unique personalities and expressions. Nadia's at home using any medium, but prefers the versatility and permanency of oils.

About Five Star Publications

Alfie's Bark Mitzvah™ is published by **Little Five Star**, a division of **Five Star Publications**. Little Five Star's mission is to help authors create books that will help children understand the implications of their life choices and help them become more tolerant and accepting of the differences in others. President Linda F. Radke, who started the firm in 1985, has worked with hundreds of authors over the years, some famous, some obscure, but all with messages they wanted others to hear. She's garnered a long list of publishing awards along the way. Five Star is one of the country's leading small press publishers, offering consulting, book production, publishing, and full marketing services. Linda was recently named "Book Marketer of the Year" by Book Publicists of Southern California.

BOOK ORDER FORM

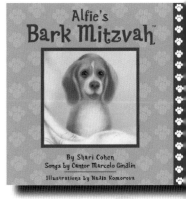

Alfie's **Bark Mitzvah**™

By Shari Cohen
Songs by Cantor Marcelo Gindlin
Illustrations by Nadia Komorova

"*Alfie's Bark Mitzvah*™ is a delight. The story and the music are wonderful. I especially love the special lessons contained in the story. This is the perfect book for little ones and their grown ups. The pictures are beautiful and engaging and really help Alfie come to life. This book is one that can be read over and over again. We read it to our dog Sophie every night and she barks with happiness. As a matter of fact, I would hope that each family has a copy of *Alfie's Bark Mitzvah*™."

Michal Marks M.A. Ed
Director of Education, Malibu Jewish Center & Synagogue

One book and CD is $18.00

Order 2 or more and get free shipping.*

Order 4 or more and receive 10% off plus free shipping.* Shipping and Handling: $5.00 for the first book and $1.00 for each additional book. Limited edition artwork available – please contact the publisher.

*Ground shipping only. Allow 1 to 2 weeks for delivery.

❑ Yes, please send me a Five Star Publications catalog.

How were you referred to Five Star Publications?

❑ Friend   ❑ Internet   ❑ Book Show   ❑ Other

Method of payment
❑ VISA ❑ Master Card ❑ Discover Card ❑ American Express

_____ _____
account number   expiration date

_____
signature

name
_____

address
_____

city, state, zip
_____

daytime phone   fax
_____

email

Item	Qty	Unit Price	Total Price

Mail or Fax your order to:
Five Star Publications, Inc.,
P.O. Box 6698
Chandler, AZ 85246-6698
Fax: 480-940-8787
Phone: 480-940-8182
Toll Free: 866-471-0777

Subtotal	
Shipping	
I bought 2 or more –ship it to me FREE!	
TOTAL	

www.AlfiesBarkMitzvah.com

Alfie's Bark Mitzvah™

*Music and lyrics by **Marcelo Gindlin***

We are so happy
'cause we're coming to celebrate –
coming to celebrate
Alfie's Bark Mitzvah!
We are surrounding him
embracing with joy and love,
coming to celebrate this special day.
Dancing in circles bringing blessings for this day.
Singing all together we can light and lift his prayers.
I am Bubbie Sarah,
I am Zayde Sam,
I am Uncle Joe,
And we wish him Mazal Tov!

You Bless My Soul

Music by **Marcelo Gindlin**
Lyrics by **Marcelo Gindlin and Michael Graubert**

Every day I thank G-d for every blessing I am grateful.
Now that you are beside me there is a holy light between us.
You helped me walk.
You helped me grow.
Your presence is changing my world.

You bless my soul with inspiration.
You bring the light from up above.
I hear your name in every heartbeat.
My soul is blessed with flowing love.

Seek G-d's face inside you.
Find your truth, your dream, your glory.
Angels will surround you
to guide the footsteps on your journey.
Bringing the joy,
singing your song,
your spirit will blossom once more.

Let's Do a Mitzvah

Music by **Marcelo Gindlin**
Lyrics by **Sue Epstein and Marcelo Gindlin**

Whenever you're lonely,
I'll give you a call.
It will make you feel happy
and then you will smile.

We can go for a walk.
We can go for a run.
We can play with my toys.
And we'll have lots of fun.

I will be your best friend
till the end of time,
and I promise to be true.
Whenever you need me,
I'll be there
and I'll sing this song for you:

Let's do a mitzvah, every day from your heart!
Let's do a mitzvah, we can all do our part!
Let's do a mitzvah, and you'll feel very good!
Let's do a mitzvah, it will come right back to you!

From Generation to Generation

Music and Lyrics by **Marcelo Gindlin**

All the traditions that we should keep
from generation to generation.
All our values, our precious gifts
from generation to generation.
Hold their hand… tell them a story.
Teach them well… sing them your melody.
It's our job to continue, to inspire our future.

From generation to generation,
we go in our lives
teaching children
helping them grow
keeping the hope alive.

When I was small I had much to learn
from generation to generation.
Learning the meaning of every day
from generation to generation.
They held my hand…told me a story.
They taught me well…sang me their melody.
And now my job is to continue, to inspire our future.

Celebration

Music and Lyrics by **Marcelo Gindlin**

This is a big day.
This is a fun day.
This a day to celebrate!

Siman Siman Tov –
Mazal Mazal Tov.

Celebration!
Celebration!

Alfie's Bark Mitzvah!
Let's sing together –
Mazal Mazal Tov!

He was a puppy.
Now he's full grown.
Mazal Mazal Tov!

Havah Nashirah Shir Halleluyah
Havah Nashirah Shir Shalom

Aleynu, Aleynu,
V'al kol ha'olam.

All songs © 2006 / Cantor Marcelo Gindlin
CREDITS
"You Bless My Soul," "Let's Do A Mitzvah," "From Generation To Generation," and "Celebration" produced and arranged by Troy Dexter and Cantor Marcelo Gindlin, and engineered, mixed, and mastered by Troy Dexter at The Green Room in Chatsworth, California in October 2006.

The song "Alfie's Bark Mitzvah" is produced and arranged by Alberto Berbara and Cantor Marcelo Gindlin, and recorded, mixed, and mastered by Troy Dexter at The Green Room in Chatsworth, California in October 2005.

LEAD VOCALS: Cantor Marcelo Gindlin ADULT CHOIR: Cantor Ruti Braier, Sue Epstein, Cantorial Soloist Lonee Frailich, Cantorial Soloist Lorna Lembeck, Jamie Rice, Cantor Wally Schachet-Briskin, Ditza Zakay CHILDREN'S CHOIR: Paulina Kurtz, Alexandra Kyman, Isaac Nassimi, Sarah Rice, Julia Wisnicki DRUMS: Robert "Jake" Jacobs GUITARS, KEYBOARDS, AND BASS: Troy Dexter SAX, CLARINET, AND FLUTE: Mike Nelson OBOE: Gary Herbig VIOLINS: Audriana Zoppo, Kathleen Robertson, Cameron Patrick VIOLA: Cameron Patrick

WHAT OTHERS ARE SAYING...

"*Alfie's Bark Mitzvah*™ is endearing and a door opener for the young about what to look forward to when the time of their Bar/Bat Mitzvah will come. It also becomes a sweet reminder for the adults of what it is all about. Shari Cohen and Cantor Marcelo Gindlin have created an imaginative-boundary pusher, caring and respectful at the same time. Nadia Komorova's charming illustrations bring Alfie and his friends to life. Cantor Marcelo Gindlin's CD of songs brings voice to Alfie. His songs are upbeat, spiritual and a delight for young and old."

Rabbi Marcelo Bronstein
Congregation B'nai Jeshurun, New York City, New York

"Cantor Marcelo Gindlin is my hero. His extraordinary voice, his generous soul, and his gift for reaching children through music comes through in every note of these wonderful songs. As a parent, I cannot thank you enough for reinforcing these lessons on mitzvot—acts of loving kindness—through your sweet, memorable compositions. My daughter, Sarah Elizabeth is singing along with you and loves the songs. On top of that, Cantor Marcelo has captured the heart of my dog, Sally, who now appears to be begging to become Bark Mitzvah, too. Truth be told, we listen to these songs so often that we can no longer tell the difference between kugel and kibble!

Julie Silver
Mother and Nationally Beloved Singer/Songwriter

"I think this book will be a wonderful way of not only introducing younger brothers and sisters to the idea of a Bar or Bat Mitzvah for their older sibling, but will help all young children look forward to the day that they too get to become Bar or Bat Mitzvah."

Rabbi Daniel Plotkin
B'nai El Congregation, St. Louis, Missouri

WHAT OTHERS ARE SAYING...cont.

"Alfie's good, forgiving and loving soul shines through these delightful pages reminding us of the purpose and spirit of Bar and Bat Mitzvahs everywhere. Mazal Tov to Shari Cohen, Cantor Marcelo Gindlin, and Nadia Komorova on this joyous book."

Leah Komaiko,
Author of numerous books for children including
Annie Bananie and *Earl's Too Cool for Me*

"I found *Alfie's Bark Mitzvah*™ story absolutely delightful!!! I enjoyed the mention of his multicultural family coming for the simcha from far and wide, including the twins, Ziv & Zev. I also felt the family's pride in Alfie's delivery, as well as his realization of the mitzvot, namely kindness to ALL others. His tale is widely appealing and both endearing and enduring because Alfie basks in the moment of this significant event, yet realizes that this marks only the beginning of his Jewish journey."

Jeannette Nemon-Fischman
Teacher, 2nd Grade, Woodland Hills, California

"Cantor Marcelo is one of the top Jewish artists in the country and *Alfie's Bark Mitzvah*™ is his best CD yet. Part musical theater and part pop, *Alfie's Bark Mitzvah*™ is 100% top notch."

Craig Taubman
Jewish Artist/ Singer/ Composer/ Producer

"Your book is beautiful to look at and filled with gentle and kind spirit. I love it! May you and Alfie go from strength to strength. Mazal Tov!"

Cantor Jay Frailich
University Synagogue, Brentwood, California

"Both touching and hilarious, this colorfully illustrated story of a dog's 'Bark Mitzvah' emphasizes the true blessings of this coming of age ritual—the study of prayers and chanting of the Torah scroll, the doing of kind deeds for others, the passing on of tradition from generation to generation, and the warm family feeling of celebration. I'm still laughing over the doggie hora dance circle!"

Rabbi Alicia Magal
Jewish Community of Sedona, Arizona

"Marcelo Gindlin makes music with love and enthusiasm. He is a treasure in the Jewish community and a serious talent. *Alfie's Bark Mitzvah*™ is fun, upbeat, and will keep you singing along."

Sam Glaser
Jewish Artist/ Singer/ Composer/ Producer

"*Alfie's Bark Mitzvah*™ is a delight. The story and the music are wonderful. I especially love the special lessons contained in the story. This is the perfect book for little ones and their grown-ups. The pictures are beautiful and engaging and really help Alfie come to life. This book is one that can be read over and over again. We read it to our dog Sophie every night and she barks with happiness. As a matter of fact, I would hope that each family has a copy of *Alfie's Bark Mitzvah*™."

Michal Marks M.A. Ed
Director of Education, Malibu Jewish Center & Synagogue, Malibu, California

WHAT OTHERS ARE SAYING...cont.

"The rhyming text and comical illustrations will appeal to all children, not just Jewish children. It also opens up discussion of other cultures which is something that all preschool teachers try to do in class. Great story!"

Rochelle Tiche
Preschool Teacher, Building Blocks Preschool, Penngrove, California

"This is a delightful tale of a puppy celebrating his becoming a Bark Mitzvah. By caring for all of G-d's creatures and by enjoying performing acts of Mitvot, Alfie is a wonderful role model for children everywhere."

Cantor Leo Fettman
Cantor and Jewish educator, Beth Israel Synagogue, Omaha, Nebraska
Cantor Fettman is the author of *Shoah: Journey from the Ashes*

"*Alfie's Bark Mitzvah*™ is a pleasure to the eye and the heart. As we watch the story of Alfie's coming-of-age unfold, we are reminded of the import and significance of our tradition's values: giving of ourselves to others, celebrating the joys of life, and the importance of Jewish ritual. With wit, charm and humor, *Alfie's Bark Mitzvah*™ is a welcome addition to every family's bookshelf and is sure to be read over and over and passed from generation to generation."

Rabbi Bryan R. Bramly
Temple Beth Sholom, Chandler, Arizona